SUPERHEROES FIGHT BULLYING WITH KINDNESS

Featuring King Elementary School Students

Do The Write Thing of DC is supported by the City Fund,
which works to make the District of Columbia a
more healthy, stable and vibrant place to live for all its residents.
The City Fund is administered by The Community Foundation for the
National Capital Region.

THECITYFUND

Text ©2017 by Carla A. Nordé and LoLo Smith
Photography © 2017 Total Entertainment Package
Illustration & Design © 2017 Gloria Marconi Illustration & Design

Printed in the United States of America
Published by: Do The Write Thing Foundation of DC

DEDICATION

FIRST GRADERS

Spirit Armstrong
Samuel Barksdale
Brian Booker-Rayfield Jr.
Kayla Brown
Serenity Brown
La'nyjah Glosson
Marjé Harris
China Hickman

Seth Horton
Makyra Johnson
Dominique Jones
Kilee Jones
Zaria Mack
Ka'niyah Moore
Alayshia Pringle-Ashby
Maniyah Smyers
Ava Toles

Sherriana Wall
Dior Webb
Jayda Young

SECOND GRADERS

Samuel Davis
Keith Robertson
Michael Smyers
William Toles

This book belongs to:

_____

ullying has become a serious problem. Many children skip school every day because they are afraid they will be bullied.

All of us must help prevent bullying. We must stop saying unkind things to one another. We must stop fighting each other. We must stop being unkind to each other on the Internet. We must learn to be kind to one another. Kindness is the new cool!

When you see the word bully, think what the letters could stand for:

 BE A FRIEND!

 USE KIND WORDS!

 LOOK FOR AND REPORT BULLYING!

 LEARN TO UNDERSTAND OTHERS.

YOU CAN STOP BULLYING.

1

SUPERMAN & SUPERGIRL

want you

to learn about bullying.

They want you

to have a plan

to stop bullying

because bullying

is not okay.

3

BATMAN & BATGIRL

say that
bullying
can happen
anywhere.
So beware!

4

5

THE FLASH & FLASHGIRL

say,

"Bullying can happen
at home, at school,
on the playground
and even on the internet."

THE FANTASTIC FOUR

(Mr. Fantastic, the Invisible Woman, the Human Torch & The Thing) say there are four types of bullying:

1. Verbal bullying
2. Physical bullying
3. Social bullying
4. Cyber bullying

9

THE INCREDIBLES

(Mister Incredible, Elastigirl, Violet, Dash and Jack-Jack) say, "Verbal bullying happens when a bully says unkind things to someone or about someone.
A bully may also call you names.
Bullying is not the same as friendly teasing."

10

CAPTAIN AMERICA & AMERICAN DREAM

say that

physical bullying means

hitting, spitting, kicking, pinching or

throwing things.

13

SPIDER-MAN & SPIDERGIRL

say social bullying means leaving others out on purpose,

spreading rumors or telling others not to be friends with someone.

14

15

WONDER WOMAN

teaches us about cyber bullying.
She says to remember
to always use kind words
on the internet.
Don't be mean behind
the computer screen!

16

ROBIN

teaches us
that there are
four roles that people play in
a bullying situation:

1. The bully

2. The victim

3. The ally

4. The bystander

THE GREEN LANTERN & GREEN LANTERN GIRL

say that a bully
is someone who tries to hurt
others. Bullies feel better
by doing unkind things.
Bullies think they are cool.
Bullies are not cool.
Be a buddy, not a bully.

20

21

HULK & SHE HULK

say that the victim of bullying
is someone who is being called names,
being hit or being left out.
A victim may have trouble sleeping,
stop doing their work at school,
become sad,
become afraid
or even want
to stop living.

23

TEENAGE MUTANT NINJA TURTLES DONATELLO

say that a victim
can be any color, size or age.
It is okay to be different.
It is NOT okay to bully
someone for being different.

24

25

TEENAGE MUTANT NINJA TURTLES
LEONARDO

say that bystanders do nothing to help a victim of bullying. That is wrong.

27

TEENAGE MUTANT NINJA TURTLES MICHELANGELO

say that the ally
is a friend of the bully.
The ally is happy to
see the bully hurt others.

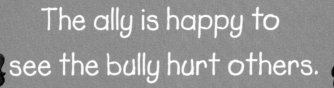

27

TEENAGE MUTANT NINJA TURTLES MICHELANGELO

say that the ally
is a friend of the bully.
The ally is happy to
see the bully hurt others.

29

TEENAGE MUTANT NINJA TURTLES
RAPHAEL

say you should help a victim by telling an adult.
If you see something, say something.
This is not tattling.

31

CAPTAIN AMERICA & AMERICAN DREAM

say you can stop being a victim

by laughing at the bully.

Ha, ha, ha, ha!

33

IRONMAN

says you can just
ignore a bully
and walk away.

34

35

GREEN LANTERN & GREEN LANTERN GIRL

say that you should ask a bully to stop.
If the bully does not stop,
you should tell your parent
or your teacher.

36

37

BATMAN & BATGIRL

want you to
BE A BUDDY, NOT A BULLY.

39

SPIDER MAN & SPIDERGIRL

say,

"IF YOU SEE SOMETHING,

SAY SOMETHING."

40

41

CAPTAIN AMERICA & AMERICAN DREAM

want you to sign the PLEDGE
TO SAY NO TO BULLYING.

42

I PLEDGE TO SAY NO TO BULLYING!

☐ I pledge to stop bullying my sister or brother at home.

☐ I pledge to stop bullying other children at school.

☐ I pledge to stop bullying other children on the playground.

☐ I pledge to stop bullying on the Internet.

☐ I pledge to tell an adult when I see someone being bullied.

☐ I pledge to say no to bullying and be like a superhero.

_____

Name

(COPY THIS PLEDGE ON A SHEET OF PAPER)

10 ACTS OF KINDNESS

The superheroes fight bullying with kindness.

**When children act kind to one another,
bullying decreases in schools.
It does not cost anything to be kind.
On the following pages are 10 acts of kindness
that children and parents can try together.**

ACT OF KINDNESS #1

Batman and Batgirl say,
"Use sidewalk chalk and write
kind messages on the sidewalk or parking lot
in your neighborhood."

A warm SMILE is the universal language of kindness.

GOOD LUCK :)

47

ACT OF KINDNESS #2

Captain America and American Dream say, "Think of three relatives that you do not see very often then write a nice, handwritten letter or card and drop it in the mail. Your letter or card will make them smile because it is rare to get a handwritten letter since most people just send texts or emails."

We RISE by lifting others.

49

ACT OF KINDNESS #3

The Flash and Flash Girl say,
"The next time that you are in a car,
wave and smile at people in other cars
to see if they will wave or smile back at you."

KINDNESS
is free.

ACT OF KINDNESS #4

The Hulk and She Hulk say,
"Take flowers to your teacher.
They are much better than apples!"

Never look
DOWN
on someone
unless
you are
helping them
UP.

53

ACT OF KINDNESS #5

Wonder Woman says,
"If you have elderly neighbors,
check in on them and
ask if you can be of any help."

No act of
KINDNESS,
no matter how
SMALL,
is ever wasted.

55

ACT OF KINDNESS #6

Spider-Man and Spider Girl say,
"Share a special toy with a friend."

Choose
KINDNESS.

ACT OF KINDNESS #7

Robin says,"Ask a parent if they
will take you to the children's hospital so you can
donate your gently used toys."

KINDNESS
is always in
season.

59

ACT OF KINDNESS #3

The Green Lantern and Green Lantern Girl say,
"Make a thank you card for your
teacher or principal."

One
KIND WORD can
change someone's
ENTIRE DAY.

61

ACT OF KINDNESS #9

Superman and Supergirl say,
"Read a book
to a younger sister or brother."

KINDNESS
is the language
which the deaf
can HEAR and the
blind can SEE.

ACT OF KINDNESS #10

Iron Man says,
"You should invite a classmate who is easily left out, to play on the playground."

It's COOL to be KIND.

65

THE KINDNESS PLEDGE

☐ I pledge to be kind to *my* family at home.

☐ I pledge to be kind to *my* classmates at school.

☐ I pledge to be kind to *my* classmates
   on the playground.

☐ I pledge to be kind to others on the Internet.

☐ I pledge to tell an adult when I see someone
   being unkind.

☐ I pledge to be a buddy, not a bully.

☐ I pledge to be a pro-kindness, anti-bullying superhero.

_____

Name

(COPY THIS PLEDGE ON A SHEET OF PAPER)

JUST FOR FUN!

TRUE OR FALSE

1. Bullying is okay.

2. Bullying can only happen in a few places.

3. Bullying can happen at home, at school, on the playground and on the Internet.

4. A type of bullying is verbal bullying.

5. Bullying is the same thing as friendly teasing.

JUST FOR FUN FACTS!

Point to the picture of the person who plays the roles in a bullying situation.

1. The person who is called names, being hit or being left out.

2. The person who tries to hurt others.

3. The person who stands by and does nothing when another person is being bullied.

4. The friend of the bully who is happy to see the bully being unkind to others.

Answers: 1. Victim 2. Bully 3. Bystander 4. Ally

NO BULLYING

By Michael Bost (*AKA* "S.W.A.G.G. BLACK")

I'm mad.
I'm mad.
I got bullies — bullies in my class.
Tryin' to study hard so I can just pass.
  I'm mad.
I got SWAGG — bullies in my class.

I'm mad.
I got SWAGG — bullies in my class.
Tryin' to study hard so I can just pass.
  I'm mad.
I got SWAGG — bullies in my class.

Bullies in my class keep on pressin' me.
They just mad at me cause I'm reachin'
  my destiny.
Is it my fault that I got a lot of SWAGG?
  (Okay, Okay)
Is it my fault I come to school? I don't DRAG.
  (No)
Now I got those bullies chasin' me
  round the block.
  (Okay, Okay)
All I want to know is when the bullying
  will stop.
And even after that they chase me
  after school,
Got me running home, saying bully rules:
  1, 2 Bully comin' for you!
                    (You)

3, 4 You betta lock your door!
                    (Wump)
5, 6 Bet not snitch!
                    (Snitch)
7, 8 Oh, bullies in yo face!
                    (In yo face)

They don't want them bullies.
I don't want them bullies.
We don't want them bullies.
We don't want them bullies.
We don't want them bullies in our schools.
We don't want them bullies in
  our neighborhoods.
We don't want them bullies.
Bully words hurt.
We don't want them bullies
  in the whole universe.

We don't want them bullies.
  (Bullies)
No bullies.
No bullying.
  (No)
This is SWAGG, SWAGG BLACK
  (No bullying)
from the planet, Swagola.
  (No bullying)
Bullying, no bullying, bullying
  (Out, out, out)

69

ABOUT THE AUTHORS

Carla A. Nordé was born and raised in the District of Columbia. After graduating from Wilson Senior High school, she worked for several years then matriculated at Trinity University for three years. She now provides consulting services to non-profits that use the arts to enhance the life success of children and youth. She is the single mother of two children, a son and daughter. She helped write this book in response to her son being bullied at school. She has written two other books, *Be A Superhero By Standing Up Against Bullying* and the Amazon #1 Bestseller *Superheroes Fight Bullying With Kindness* with LoLo Smith.

LoLo Smith is an educator, writer and creator of Living Storybook, a literacy and performing arts program for young children. She has written three other books, *Mr. Jordan Goes To Washington*, *I Know My Community Workers* and *Sista CindyElla Mae*, the African-American re-telling of the Cinderella story. She was raised and educated in St. Louis but has lived in Washington, D.C. for over forty years. She has one adult son.

ABOUT THE PHOTOGRAPHER

Tep Gardner is an award-winning photographer with 45 years of experience. He is a green screen expert who specializes in portraits, special events and fashion shoots. Contact him at 202.239.0643 or email: tepentertainment@gmail.com.

ABOUT THE DESIGNER

Gloria Marconi is an illustrator and graphic designer who has been working in the Washington, DC area for nearly 50 years. A multi-faceted artist, Ms. Marconi specializes in print and works in a variety of media ranging from traditional to quilting to computer-generated illustration. Over the years, her clients have run the gamut from corporations to government to non-profits as well as editorial illustrations for books, magazines and advertising. She lives in suburban Maryland and can be reached at gmarconidesign@verizon.net.

CPSIA information can be obtained
at www.ICGtesting.com
Printed in the USA
LVOW06*0915020717
540113LV00018B/178/P

9 781532 338472